READING CHAMPION

The Giant Snowball Mystery

by A.H. Benjamin and Andy Rowland

FRANKLIN WATTS
LONDON • SYDNEY

Rabbit woke up and jumped out of bed.

He looked out of the window.

It was a beautiful winter morning.

Everything was covered in white.

Rabbit ran out of his house
and up the hill to play in the snow.
"Whoopee!" he shouted. "This is fun!"
Just then, he saw a giant snowball
rolling down the hill ...

"Oh, no!" cried Rabbit.

He jumped out of the way, just in time!

The giant snowball rolled past.

"Where did that come from?" asked Rabbit.

He ran after it.

A little way down the hill, Mole had just come out of her house to sweep her path. "What a lovely morning!" she said.

Then she looked up the hill
and saw the giant snowball
coming towards her.

"Help!" cried Mole.

She ran back into her house, just in time.

The giant snowball rolled past
with Rabbit chasing after it.

Mole poked her head out of the door.

"What was that?" she asked.

"I don't know," puffed Rabbit.

"Come on, let's find out."

They both hurried after the giant snowball.

The sun was shining through the window.

It woke Squirrel up from her winter sleep.

She stretched her paws and yawned.

"I'm hungry," she said.

She climbed down the tree to get
some nuts from her store.
"Yum, yum!" she said as she nibbled.
Suddenly, the giant snowball appeared.

"Look out, Squirrel!" cried Rabbit.

Squirrel scampered up the tree,

just in time.

The giant snowball rolled past.

"Goodness me!" said Squirrel.

"What was that?" she asked.

"We don't know," said Mole.

"But we are going to find out,"
said Rabbit.

"I'll come with you," said Squirrel,
and she scampered down the tree.

Soon Rabbit, Mole and Squirrel caught up
with the giant snowball.
It had stopped in a big field.
"Wow!" they gasped. "It's so BIG!"

Just then the snowball began to shake.

Everyone stepped back.

Suddenly, the giant snowball burst open
and out popped ... Badger!

"Surprise!" he laughed.

Everyone gasped.

"How did you get in there?" they asked.

"I'll show you," said Badger.

Badger took them up to the top of the hill.

"Look," he said, "all I did was ..."

Story order

Look at these 5 pictures and captions.
Put the pictures in the right order
to retell the story.

1

The animals chase the snowball.

2

Badger shakes off the snow.

3

Rabbit wakes to find snow everywhere.

4

Badger shows the others what he did.

5

A snowball is heading towards Mole.

Independent Reading

This series is designed to provide an opportunity for your child to read on their own. These notes are written for you to help your child choose a book and to read it independently.

In school, your child's teacher will often be using reading books which have been banded to support the process of learning to read. Use the book band colour your child is reading in school to help you make a good choice. *The Giant Snowball Mystery* is a good choice for children reading at Purple Band in their classroom to read independently.

The aim of independent reading is to read this book with ease, so that your child enjoys the story and relates it to their own experiences.

About the book
Rabbit awakes to find everything covered in snow. Suddenly a giant snowball shoots past! Rabbit sets out to investigate, along with his friends Mole and Squirrel.

Before reading
Help your child to learn how to make good choices by asking: "Why did you choose this book? Why do you think you will enjoy it?" Look at the cover together and ask: "What do you think the story will be about?" Ask your child to think of what they already know about the story context. Then ask your child to read the title aloud. Ask: "It's called 'The Giant Snowball Mystery' – what is a mystery story?" Remind your child that they can sound out the letters to make a word if they get stuck.

Decide together whether your child will read the story independently or read it aloud to you.

During reading

Remind your child of what they know and what they can do independently. If reading aloud, support your child if they hesitate or ask for help by telling the word. If reading to themselves, remind your child that they can come and ask for your help if stuck.

After reading

Support comprehension by asking your child to tell you about the story. Use the story order puzzle to encourage your child to retell the story in the right sequence, in their own words. The correct sequence can be found on the next page.

Help your child think about the messages in the book that go beyond the story and ask: "What do the animals think of the snow? How would you react?"

Give your child a chance to respond to the story: "What was your favourite part? Why do you think the animals chased the snowball?"

Extending learning

Help your child think more about the inferences in the story by asking: "What do you think the animals will do next? Why do you think that?"

In the classroom, your child's teacher may be teaching how to use speech marks to show when characters are speaking. There are many examples in this book that you could look at with your child. Find these together and point out how the end punctuation (comma, full stop, question mark or exclamation mark) comes inside the speech mark. Ask the child to read some examples out loud, adding appropriate expression.

Franklin Watts
First published in Great Britain in 2018
by The Watts Publishing Group

Series Editors: Jackie Hamley and Melanie Palmer
Series Advisors: Dr Sue Bodman and Glen Franklin
Series Designer: Peter Scoulding

A CIP catalogue record for this book is
available from the British Library.

ISBN 978 1 4451 6224 9 (hbk)
ISBN 978 1 4451 6225 6 (pbk)
ISBN 978 1 4451 6226 3 (library ebook)

Printed in China

Franklin Watts
An imprint of
Hachette Children's Group
Part of The Watts Publishing Group
Carmelite House
50 Victoria Embankment
London EC4Y 0DZ

An Hachette UK Company
www.hachette.co.uk

www.franklinwatts.co.uk

Answer to Story order: 3, 5, 1, 2, 4